EGYPTIAN TALES

THE MAGIC AND THE MUMMY

Bloomsbury Education
An imprint of Bloomsbury Publishing Plc

50 Bedford Square
London
WC1B 3DP
UK

1385 Broadway
New York
NY 10018
USA

www.bloomsbury.com

BLOOMSBURY and the Diana logo are trademarks of Bloomsbury Publishing Plc

First published in Great Britain 2011
This paperback edition published in 2017

ISBN
PB: 978 1 4729 4216 6
epub: 978 1 4759 5253 0
epdf: 978 1 4729 5252 3

2 4 6 8 10 9 7 5 3 1

Typeset by Newgen Knowledge Works (P) Ltd., Chennai, India

Printed and bound in UK by CPI Group (UK) ltd, Croydon CR0 4YY

TERRY DEARY

EGYPTIAN TALES

THE MAGIC AND THE MUMMY

Illustrated by Helen Flook

BLOOMSBURY EDUCATION
AN IMPRINT OF BLOOMSBURY
LONDON OXFORD NEW YORK NEW DELHI SYDNEY

CHAPTER 1
The House of Death

Neria couldn't sleep.

She lay on the cool floor of her room and wriggled with excitement.

"The House of Death!" she whispered in the dark. "The House of Death!" And she remembered over and over again what her father had told her the night before.

"Neria," he said. "You are a clever girl."

"Thank you Father," she muttered and blushed. He hardly ever seemed to notice her. He was a grand priest at the royal temple. He certainly hadn't told her she was clever before. How did he know?

He dusted crumbs of bread off his hands and wiped his thin mouth. His scary, dark eyes looked into her. "I can trust you," he went on.

"Oh, yes, Father," she said quietly.

"I have a very special task for you," he said. Her brothers and sisters fell silent and looked at her.

She was the oldest and they always knew she was a special girl. She was like a mother to them since their own mother had died a year ago. Their faces were still but their ears were twitching like hippos on the banks of the Nile.

Neria nodded.

"Tomorrow I am taking you to the House of Death with me," the man said. His shaved head glowed in the golden light of the oil lamps and he looked like a god.

"Oooh!" her youngest brother, Karu, cried. "House of Death! Neria is going to die."

The priest turned his head slowly and looked at his little son. The boy gave a hiccup of fear. "The House of Death is not the place you go to die, my son. It is the place you go after you are dead... at least the place the great people of Egypt go when they are dead."

The little boy's mouth fell open. "Oooh!"

"The House of Death is where we preserve the bodies of people..."

"What's 'preserve'?" Karu whispered.

Father nodded. "If you have a piece of meat, and you leave it in the sun, what happens to it?"

"The cat would pinch it!" the little boy said.

"Or the jackals would come in from the desert and gobble it up."

Father closed his eyes for a moment and took a slow breath. "If you put it on the roof, where the cats and the jackals couldn't get it..."

Karu wriggled. "The birds would eat it."

The priest held the table so tightly his knuckles turned white. Neria tried to shake her head – to tell her little brother to close his mouth before their father lost his temper.

At last their father said. "If we put the meat in a cage, and close the door, so the animals and birds could not eat it, what would happen to it?"

Karu smiled. "Then I would open the door of the cage and I would eat it!"

"No you would NOT!" their father shouted. The children jumped as if a Nile crocodile had snapped its jaws suddenly shut. "I will TELL you what would happen to the meat. It would become slimy and very smelly. It would be covered in flies and the flies would lay their eggs. The eggs would hatch out into maggots and the maggots would eat the meat."

"Do they like slimy, smelly meat?" the boy gasped.

"They *love* it," Father said. "Love it." He turned back to Neria. "People like us would be like pieces of meat when we died. We'd rot and smell and be eaten by maggots. That is why we have to turn people into mummies."

"I know, Father," Neria said.

"That's what we do in the House of Death. We make mummies." He lowered his voice. "We are going to get very busy in the House of Death some day soon. I need some extra help. Someone who can learn quickly. Someone I can trust. I have chosen you, Neria."

The girl felt a warm tingle in her cheeks. "Thank you, Father," she said and lowered her dark eyes.

In the quiet of the room little Karu's voice sounded like a reed pipe. "Will I be made into a mummy, Father, or will I be eaten by maggots?"

Father turned on him with an angry glare. "If you do not close your monkey mouth you will be chopped up and fed to the crocodiles."

"Ooooh!" Karu cried. He jumped to his feet in fear, took a step backwards and fell over the cat. The cat squawked, the boy squeaked and the children tried to hide their laughter.

"Get to bed NOW!" Father roared. "Or I will feed you to the pharaoh's own pet crocodile."

Karu fled, his little legs pattering faster than his thumping heart. He clutched his favourite rag ball to his mouth.

Neria was sure Father's tight mouth was trying not to laugh. At last he looked around the table. "In fact you can all go to bed," he said. "Sleep well, Neria. You have a busy day ahead tomorrow."

But Neria didn't sleep well. She hardly slept at all. Her cat crept onto her blanket and purred like a mountain lion.

She stroked it and whispered, "The House of Death! I'm going to the House of Death, Katkins."

The cat purred.

At last the black night turned to the darkest grey and she knew Horus the Hawk God was opening his eye. The eye that was the sun.

It was time to go.

CHAPTER 2
Fate of the Pharaoh

Neria's father was dressed in his finest robes today. He marched down the middle of the road and everyone scurried to get out of his way. It was as if he was too bright to look at; bright as the eye

of Horus. Even the dogs tucked in their tails and ran.

Neria walked a little way behind him. Suddenly a woman ran out from a dark doorway. She threw her arms up to the sky and shrieked. Then she bent down to the ground, grabbed a fistful of dust and let it trickle over her grey-black hair.

Neria's father nodded. "So, it has started. We must hurry." He strode out and the girl trotted to his side.

"What has started, Father?"

"The woman must have heard some news. Last night the pharaoh was sick. This morning he must be dead." He marched on. "We have work to do."

They headed east towards the rising sun, passed through the poorer streets of shambling houses and then through the city gates. Guards raised their spears to salute them.

Neria copied her father; she raised her chin and ignored them.

This gate led into the desert and ahead of them stood the House of Death. Not a house at all. A fine white tent that had no walls. All the smells could be blown away on the desert breeze. Perfumes of cedar and rose took away the smell of death but still the jackals on the hills caught the scent. They watched and waited.

Inside the House of Death dozens of men and women hurried about their tasks. When Neria's father came near they stopped and bowed.

There were twenty tables under the rippling white roof and every one had a body on it. The priest walked up to a man in a black robe and said, "Has it started, Thekel?"

Thekel was a large man with a small, round head. It was shaved and his ears stuck out like handles on a water jug. He smiled happily.

"It has started, Lord. The old pharaoh became a god last night at moonrise. They're dumping his body here later on today."

Neria's father pulled a face as if cheerful Thekel's words had hurt. He turned and said, "This is my daughter, Neria. She'll deal with Bastet."

Neria was puzzled. She knew that Bastet was the cat-god who looked after their corn.

Thekel grinned his simple grin. "We need all the hands we can get."

"Teach her what to do," her father ordered.

"Leave it to me. Let's start with the brain-pulling, shall we?" he asked.

Before Neria could answer, her father said, "No! Wait. If the pharaoh's body is arriving this afternoon we need to get Nesumontu out of the way. Let's do it now."

Thekel winked at Neria. "Won't be long, Mistress. I'll have him gutted in no time."

He clapped his hands and the priests gathered around. "Right, My Lords. We need to get Nesumontu ripped open. Let's make it snappy... as the crocodile said to the fish."

The priests shuffled around one table where the body of a withered old man lay. They began to chant a prayer and their voices filled the tent.

They looked to the east where light from the eye of Horus was pouring into the tent.

Neria shuddered when she saw the great god Anubis walk out of the sun and towards the body. He had the body of a man but the big-eared, sharp-nosed head of a monstrous jackal.

Neria had expected to see the dead here. But this was a shock. This was Anubis... the God of the Dead himself.

CHAPTER 3
The First Mummy

Anubis walked between the tables and stumbled. He caught his toe on the leg of a table. The leg cracked, the table fell and the mummy of a man rolled onto the floor.

"Ohhhh!" Anubis roared with pain and anger. He raised his hands, grasped his ears and pulled. Neria blinked as Anubis pulled his head off.

But the head of Anubis was just a mask. Under the mask was the red and angry face of her father. "I hate this mask," he grumbled as the chanting of the priests became a jumble of noise and stuttered to an end. "Can't see a blind thing."

He threw the mask to the ground and limped to the table where the old man's body lay. "Has someone scooped out the brain?"

A young priest held up a bowl of grey mush. "Yes, Lord."

"We're in a hurry," Neria's father said. He looked at the body. "Sorry, Nesumontu," he sighed. "I'll have to do you without the mask."

A priest handed Neria's father a pen made from a reed and a pot of ink. He marked a line about the length of his hand on the old man's side and then turned to the man in black. "Right, Thekel, get on with it!"

Thekel took a sharp stone knife from his belt and sliced along the line her father had just drawn. He plunged his hand into the body, wriggled it around and quickly pulled out the stomach. A priest took it and wrapped it in a cloth. He took it off to a stone jar and plopped it in.

They did the same with the liver, kidneys, lungs and guts. When Thekel was finished, the priests began to jeer at him.

Thekel grinned and said, "Thanks, lads. But can we cut it short? We're in a hurry today."

"Oh, all right," they agreed and went back to their jobs.

Thekel turned to Neria. "Right Mistress, I need to give you a quick lesson in making a mummy."

"But why did they call you all those names?" she asked. "Didn't you mind?"

"Nah!" he chuckled. "It's an unclean job. I do it and they have to drive me out of the House of Death because I am an unclean man. Just a sort of game really. Now I'll just wash the blood off my hands and I'll show you around."

By the end of the morning Neria knew most of the things that went on in the House of Death. The bodies that had been emptied, like old Nesumontu's, were washed with palm wine – inside and out and then they were ready to be dried out.

"We cover the body in this salty stuff –

natron," Thekel explained. "We leave it for forty days until it's dry as a desert beetle's back, and then we wrap it in bandages to make a mummy."

Neria nodded towards a boy who was writing on parchment pieces. "What's he doing?"

"Writing the Book of the Dead – prayers that are wrapped in the bandages. They help the dead person in the next life. The gods must be clever enough to read them. I never learned to read or write."

"Neither did I," Neria said.

"Never mind," Thekel shrugged. "You won't have to. Here is your table. All you have to do is turn Bastet into a mummy."

Neria was just about to ask, "Who's Bastet?" when she heard a loud noise and it was getting louder. "What's that sound?"

"Trumpets," Thekel said. "The pharaoh is coming. Here we go! Stand by your tables, lads!"

CHAPTER 4
Cruel for Cats

Soldiers marched into the tent carrying the pharaoh in a cloth cradle slung between two poles.

Neria's father met the men and led them to an empty table. The girl saw that a cat was marching with the soldiers, tail held high and proud as if it was the pharaoh himself.

Suddenly Thekel swooped and picked up the startled cat. He carried it carefully over to Neria's table. "Here you are, Mistress. This is Bastet. It is your job to turn him into a mummy."

"The cat? The pharaoh named his cat after the god? And you want me to turn it into a mummy?"

"Of course. The pharaoh had his holy cat when he was alive. He has to have it with him in his tomb. They will go to the Afterlife together."

Neria blinked. "I know animal mummies go in tombs with their masters – but this one is still alive. I can't turn a live cat into a mummy."

Thekel grinned his wide and happy grin. "I know."

"So, what do I do?" Neria frowned.

"Kill it!"

The cat was the colour of warm sand and its eyes were as pure as gold. It stood on her table and looked up at her. It stretched its neck and rubbed its head against her chin. It looked just like Katkins.

"Here's my knife," Thekel said.

Neria took the cold, black blade. The cat purred. Tears began to prickle her eyes. "I – I can't!"

Thekel shrugged. "You have to. Your father will be very upset if the pharaoh's cat doesn't go into the tomb with him."

"I can't," Neria said stupidly. "What am I going to do?"

The big man with the small head looked at her tenderly. "You know the story of Osiris? The first mummy?"

Neria nodded. "Osiris was killed by his brother and chopped into 13 pieces. His wife gathered all the pieces together and used magic to bring him back to life for a little while. And then she wrapped the 13 pieces as a mummy so his spirit could go to the Afterlife."

Thekel shook his head. "Not exactly. His wife only found 12 pieces. A crocodile had eaten one! So she replaced the lost bit with a piece of wood." He lowered his voice. "We do it in here – if an arm falls off we replace it with a piece of wood. We wrap it in bandages and no one ever notices."

The cat purred and looked up at the man. Neria stroked it and frowned. "So?"

"What if we lost a whole body – or a whole cat?" he whispered.

"You'd... you'd have to wrap up a whole mummy full of wood," she breathed.

Thekel spread his hands wide, grinned and said nothing. He looked at the cat. The cat looked back.

Neria snatched the cat from the table, tucked it under her arm and ran from the tent. Everyone was fussing about the pharaoh. No one but Thekel saw her go.

She raced across the desert, through the city gate, down the crowded street and into her house.

Neria dropped the grumbling cat into a wooden chest in her room. A moment later she was back to drop in a piece of dried fish and then closed the lid.

She raced around the house and gathered up anything useful she could find – wooden spoons and even Karu's wooden crocodile on wheels. She still needed something round, and about the size of her fist, to make the head.

Karu was playing in the garden alone. He was throwing his rag ball up in the air and catching it. "Karu!" Neria cried. "Throw me your ball."

The little boy shook his head. "No. It's my ball."

"I'll show you a wonderful game."

"No," he said and stuck out his bottom lip.

Neria knew she didn't have much time. "I'll... I'll use magic and turn it into something wonderful!"

Karu narrowed his eyes. "What?"

"A cat! A cat like my Katkins. You've always wanted one."

"You can't do magic," the little boy sniffed.

"Urrrrgh!" Neria cried angrily. She marched up to Karu, snatched the ball from his podgy little hand and ran.

She was racing down the road and could hear his wailing until she was half way to the city gates.

CHAPTER 5
The Magic Cat

As the eye of Horus sank in the sky the desert grew dark with purple shadows. Neria trotted back home behind her Father. "You did well," he said.

"Thank you father," she said.

"The mummy you made from the cat Bastet was fine – for a first try."

"Thank you Father."

"Very neat."

They walked through the city gates. The guards saluted and closed the gates to shut out the jackals of the night. When they reached their house, Karu was waiting for them. His scowling face was streaked with mud and tears.

Father ignored him. The boy cried out, "Father, Father! Neria stole my ball –

she took it and she..." Karu stopped shouting. It's hard to shout when your big sister has a hand across your mouth.

She dragged the boy down the hall and into her room. Karu struggled all the way. There was just enough light in her room to see the chest in the corner. She took her hand away from her brother's mouth.

"Where's my ball?" he sobbed.

"I haven't got it."

"Waaaagh! Why not?"

"I told you," she hissed. "I used magic to turn it into a cat."

Karu stopped crying suddenly. "No you didn't."

"Yes I did."

"Where is it?" he demanded.

"In that chest," she said.

He ran over to the corner of the room and heaved up the lid. A dazed cat blinked up at him. "Ohhhh!" Karu breathed. "A cat."

"Your cat," Neria told him.

Karu lifted the cat out carefully and clutched it in his short arms. "A magic cat," he said.

Neria smiled. "A magic cat. Now let's wash your face and go to dinner."

As the servants lit the lamps in the dining room Karu walked in with a scrubbed and happy face. "Neria," he said.

"Yes, Karu?"

"I think you stole my crocodile on wheels."

"So?"

"So I would like you to magic me a bow and arrow, a fishing boat and a golden bowl for my cat."

Neria smiled sweetly at her brother. "Karu. You have your cat. Ask me for anything else and I will turn you into a mummy."

"You can't do that!" he squawked.

"Oh, yes I can — Father says I make a fine mummy, a neat mummy."

Her teeth and eyes glinted in the lamplight. Karu looked up at her and was afraid. He swallowed hard, turned pale and began to shake.

"It's alright, Neria. You can keep my crocodile," he said.

"I think that's best," she said softly. "Mummy knows best."

AFTERWORD

The House of Death was a large tent where a mummy was made ready for its last journey – the journey into the Afterlife. It was both a holy place and a work place.

The priest in charge was a servant of the jackal god, Anubis, who was thought to watch over mummies and guard their tombs. This priest led the chanting of prayers, and really did wear a jackal mask over his head.

It is also true that a pharaoh could not go into the Afterlife without his loyal pets. They had to be killed and turned into mummies too, so they could be buried with him. Poor pets!